This book is dedicated to
MAUDIE, **B**ARCLAY,
MANDU
& **L**AIKA

Лайка = Laika
pronounced like+(a)

A TEMPLAR BOOK

First published in the UK in 2013 by Templar Publishing
This softback edition published in 2014 by Templar Publishing,
an imprint of The Templar Company Limited,
Deepdene Lodge, Deepdene Avenue,
Dorking, Surrey, RH5 4AT, UK
www.templarco.co.uk

Copyright © 2013 by Owen Davey

First edition

All rights reserved

ISBN 978-1-78370-027-1

Edited by Libby Hamilton

Printed in Singapore

Picture credit: page 32
photograph of Laika
copyright © Mary
Evans Picture
Library/Epic

templar publishing

Laika was a stray dog,
wandering the streets of Moscow.
She had no family and nowhere to call home.

1957

Laika was all alone.

At night she looked at the stars and made a wish –
a wish to find a family who would love her.

Then someone
noticed Laika was alone
and decided she would be perfect
for a very special job...

A group of scientists wanted her to try out their new spacecraft. She trained very hard and was tested many times until finally...

Laika was ready to go into space.
She climbed aboard her rocket and waited.

10... 9... 8... 7... 6... 5... 4... 3... 2... 1...

00:0

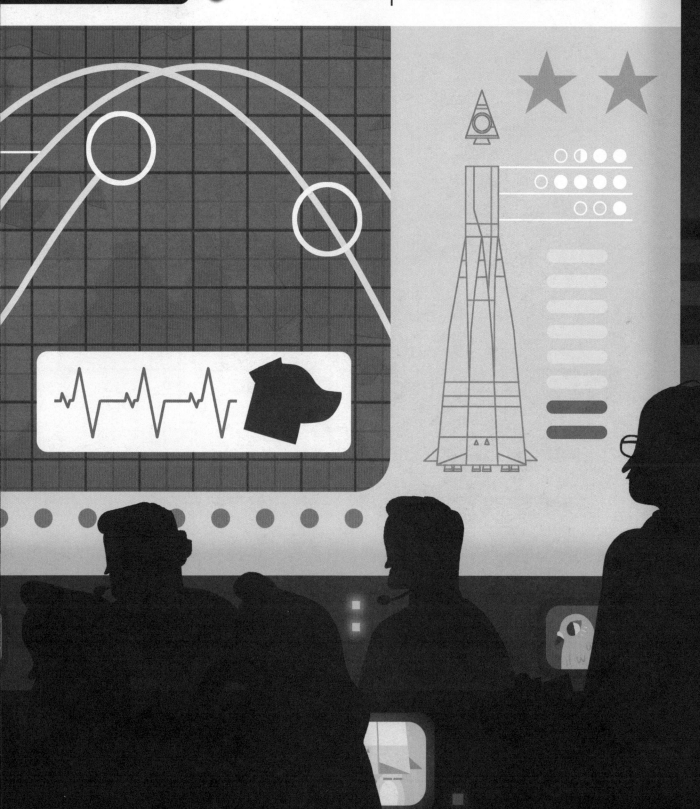

The whole world watched as little Laika zoomed up towards the stars.

6:17

Laika's spaceship circled the Earth. Now everyone knew her name, but she felt more alone than ever.

Then her rocket started making funny noises.
Something had gone wrong.

5:08

Back at mission control, the screens went blank.
Everyone on Earth thought Laika was lost.

In the years that followed,
people wrote books about her, made stamps with
her face on them and even put up a statue of her.

The brave little dog, whose journey into space
paved the way for people to follow,
would never be forgotten.

But Laika was not lost at all.
Laika had been found.

She had been rescued from the broken spaceship and
taken far away from the lonely life she had known…

... by the loving family
she had always dreamed
of finding.

A note from the author:

On November 3, 1957, Laika became the first
animal to orbit Earth when she was launched into
space in the *Sputnik 2* rocket. Laika's brave journey
paved the way for humankind to follow.

A few hours later, her spacecraft malfunctioned
and most people think that Laika was lost.
This story, with its happy ending fit for a
true explorer, is the one I choose to believe.